To Ellie,

Love from,

Teacher Jackie

"Sweet little Ellie,
time to shut your eyes.
The moon has come out,
there are stars in the skies."

"But I'm not very tired;
I don't want to count sheep.
I wonder how all of my friends
get to sleep?"

"That's a good question.
Well, why don't we see?
Hold my hand tightly, Ellie,
stay close to me."

"Here are the ducklings
wading out of the lake.
They're all nice and clean
and now barely awake!"

"Deer share happy thoughts.
It makes them all smile.
They'll settle down
then be asleep
in a while."

"These hedgehogs are S-T-R-E-T-C-H-I-N-G
It's the start of their day.
At bedtime they'll end it
the very same way!"

"Do you hear lullabies
as the baby birds sing?
Soon they'll be dreaming
beneath Mom's soft wing."

"The squirrels like stories
at bedtime, it seems.
I'll bet it's a tale that will
give them sweet dreams."

"The cotton-tailed bunnies
love cuddling up tight.
They'll hug till they're snug
then they'll snooze through the night."

Now Ellie is sleepy.
The moon's in the sky.
"Please can I have
a good night lullaby?"

"Sweet little Ellie,
I hope you sleep tight.
May you dream the most
beautiful dreams.
Night night..."